The Camel Driver's Helper

by
Terry Parker

The Camel Driver's Helper

Publishing services provided by Fitting Words LLC—www.fittingwords.net

Illustrations by Sarah Grace Wright
Cover design provided by Lillian Abernathy—www.lacreative09.com

ISBN-13: 978-1-7357748-0-0
Library of Congress Cataloging-in-Publication Data

Printed in the United States of America

The Camel Driver's Helper

Other Books
by Terry Parker

A Shepherd's Christmas Story
Sarah's Easter Miracle
The Robert P. Rabbit Series
Book One - Katie, Will and the Global Detectives
Book Two - The Moon Rock Mystery
Book Three - The Treasure of Long John Silver IV

This story is dedicated to Brad and Nancy Allen, who, by example, display the true joy of giving their best to Jesus.

Table of Contents

Chapter 1 1

Chapter 2 11

Chapter 3 19

Chapter 4 25

Chapter 5 33

Chapter 6 41

Chapter 7 49

About the Author. 57

Chapter 1

"**M**ista, I don't know if we should be doing this. What if the officials see us? You will lose your status as a midwife," Carly said, trying to be as quiet as she could, even though no one was anywhere near the two of them as they crouched in the shadow of the broom tree.

They had put the baby boy carefully into the basket and laid it beside the road so the camel driver would be sure to see him.

Mista was one of the most respected women in this part of Jerusalem, as she had been delivering babies for mothers of all faiths, and had seen the birth of hundreds of Jewish children over the years. But this child seemed special to her, so she wanted it to be taken by very loving parents. The mother of the child was the wife of a poor worker who helped harvest figs, a grueling and difficult job that was very seasonal, meaning that he only made money during the harvest season. The parents had told Mista that they couldn't afford to raise another child and asked her to see if she could find someone else to raise the boy. Normally, this would not have been hard for Mista, but this child had a disability that might make it hard to find a home for him.

"Oh dear," Carly said. "I don't think that is the camel driver coming." She and Mista were watching a man coming down the road on a donkey. They had not been expecting anyone this early except the camel driver.

As he approached the basket, the man on the donkey looked down and stopped. Mista's heart stopped too. She saw him climb down from the donkey, reach into the basket, and pick up the baby. Mista thought about crying out, but just before she did, the man put the baby down on the road, picked up the basket, got back on his donkey, and continued his journey.

"Did you see that?" Carly said. "He stole the basket—and just left the baby on the side of the road to die. How terrible!"

"But if he was going to take anything, I'm glad it was just the basket," Mista said.

"What should we do now?" Carly asked.

"Nothing," Mista said, "because I'm sure the camel driver will be along soon. He and his wife will be leading their camels rather than riding them, as they have just finished a long trip and will want to rest the camels, so he will surely see the baby."

The camel driver, Bendar, and his wife, Marca, were a middle-aged couple. They lived south of Babylon, in Nippur, which lay between the Tigris and Euphrates Rivers far to the east of Jerusalem. They had been leading caravans of merchants for many years from Babylon in the east to Egypt in the west, and Mista knew that on this early morning they would be coming down the road on the way to pick up some travelers in Jericho. Then they would all head to the Fertile Crescent to buy spices.

Mista had gotten to know both Bendar and Marca many years ago when someone on one of their caravans had needed a midwife to deliver a baby. Since that time, whenever they came through Jerusalem, Marca would stop to have a meal with Mista and Carly. While they ate, Marca would share stories of her travels, which Carly dearly loved to hear since she had never been farther away from Jerusalem than the Dead Sea.

From these conversations, Mista had learned that Marca dearly wanted a child but was never able to have a baby. When Mista heard that Marca's cousin had just had a baby and was traveling with them on this trip to return to their family in Babylon, she knew exactly what she needed to do. But she and Carly decided they wouldn't go directly to Marca, as then it would be too easy for Bendar to just say no. If, instead, Marca found the baby in a basket by the side of the road, they figured it would be very difficult for Bendar to decide to walk away and leave the boy to die.

So Mista and Carly held their breaths as Bendar and Marca and half a dozen camels came down the road toward the sleeping baby.

"Bendar," Marca exclaimed. "Is that what I think it is? It looks like a baby—and there is no one around. It's just all by itself. The poor thing."

3

"It's none of our business," Bendar said. "I'm sure someone will be coming back to get it straight away."

"But we can't just walk by without checking on it," Marca said. "What if it fell out of someone's cart? The mother will be sick with worry. We need to pick it up and make sure it is all right."

She added, "We should stay here for a while until the mother returns."

"Marca, we have to pick up our travelers this morning. Remember, we told them we would be there by lunchtime."

"Oh, Bendar, lunchtime is hours away. Surely we can wait here for a little while."

Before Bendar could answer, Marca had stooped down and picked up the baby.

"Oh, Bendar, he's a boy," she said as she unwrapped the baby's blanket. "And look how calm he is. Sleeping like a baby."

"Well, of course he's sleeping like a baby," Bendar said. "He is a baby."

"Most babies would be crying, being all alone and out here on a busy road," Marca said.

Just then Bendar got a good look at the baby, and he noticed the boy's disability.

"Marca, I don't think anyone is coming back for this baby. I think he was left here on purpose."

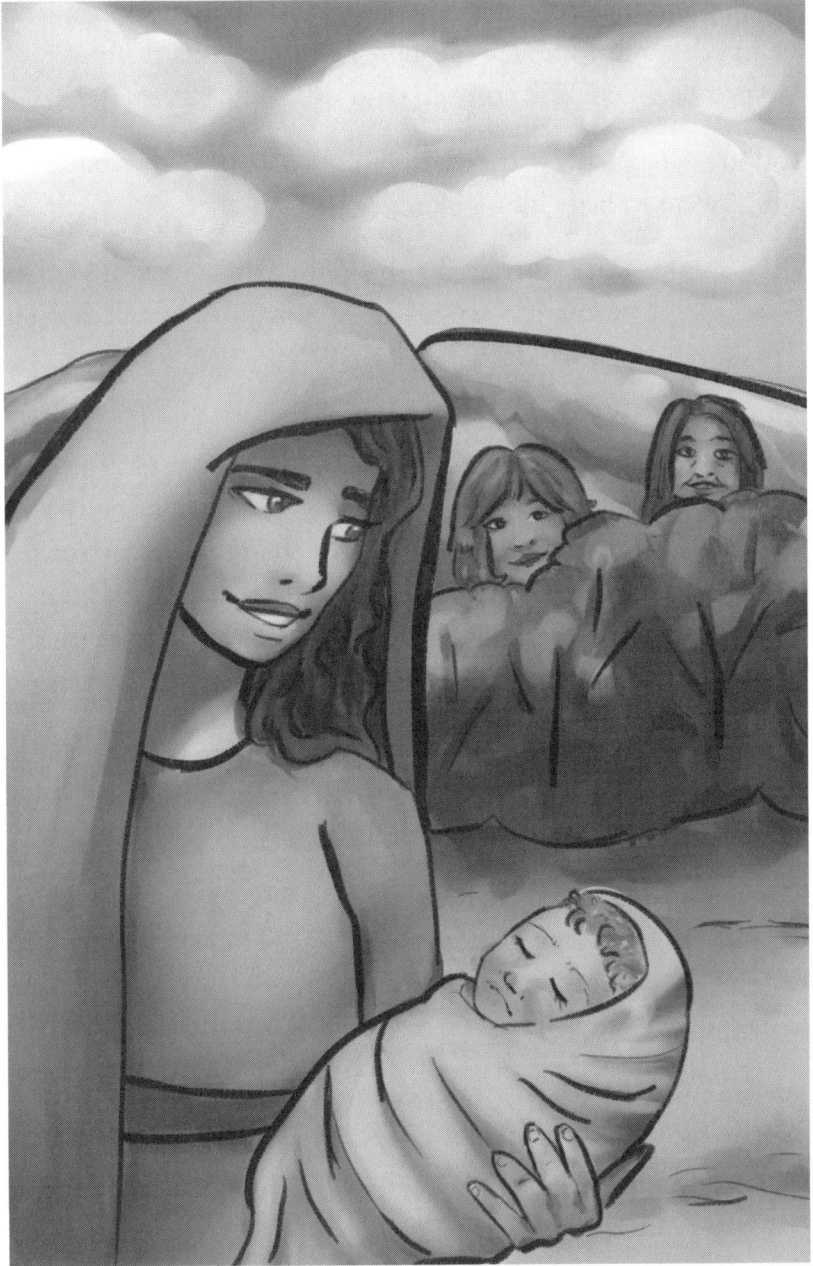

At that moment, the baby woke up, smiled at Marca, and wrapped his little fingers around her thumb, as if to say, "I want to be yours. Will you keep me?"

"I don't care what's wrong with him. If no one comes back for him, I want to keep him," Marca said.

"But, Marca, can't you see that his right arm is half missing?" Bendar said. "How can we raise a boy with only half a right arm and no right hand?"

"Oh Bendar, that's all the more reason we should keep him," she said. "We've always wanted a child, and now God has, in His providence, given us one. And just think, He has given us one that needs us so much more than a child that has two arms. God has entrusted us with a special child that I know He has a special purpose for, and we will just have to take care of the child to see what that purpose is. Then we will rejoice when we see it."

"Marca, I don't know," Bendar said. "I guess we can't just leave him here to die, but how will we feed him?"

"My cousin just had a baby, and it will take us weeks to get back to Babylon, so we can ask her if she will feed this child along with her own. Remember, Bendar, she is family, so I know she will do it, and especially since she understands the needs of a child."

So as Mista and Carly hugged each other and cried, they watched the precious baby being carried away in the arms of Marca and the camel driver to the special destiny God had in store for this one-armed little boy.

The trip back to Nippur seemed like a dream come true for Marca. At last she had a baby of her own to love and care for. She couldn't wait to show all her family and friends what a great blessing had come her way. And when they arrived home, Marca's cousin was more than happy to continue feeding the new baby, as she had become very attached to him while on the trip. She had several children of her own, so she spent as much of her time as necessary teaching Marca how to raise and care for a child.

They named the baby Ezra, since he had been born in Jerusalem, and they were told that Ezra was a good Jewish name.

At first, Marca was very careful with Ezra since he was missing most of his right arm, but Bendar insisted that they treat him just like all the other children and make him do the same things they did. In this way, Ezra became very, very good at any task using his left arm and hand and the "special right-side tool," which was the name that they gave to his short right arm.

Whenever Ezra had trouble doing a simple task because he was trying to use just his left arm and hand, Marca would say, "Ezra, use your special tool; that's what God gave it to you for." And Ezra would quickly learn that with his special tool, he could do almost anything any other child could do.

As Ezra grew older, boys would sometimes try to bully him. But they quickly found out that Ezra was twice as strong in his left arm than they expected because he had to use it so much. They also couldn't protect themselves from Ezra's "special tool," since they had never dealt with such a thing from anyone

else they had bullied. So, they left Ezra be. This was perfectly okay with him because his real love was the camels, and he wanted to spend as much time with them as he could.

That's why Ezra became the camel driver's helper at a very young age. By the time he was a teenager, Ezra had traveled through all of Babylonia, Assyria, Israel, and Egypt, riding, leading, packing, feeding, and taking care of camels in every way.

Chapter 2

As a camel driver's helper, the trips that Ezra looked forward to the most were any that went through Jerusalem. His mother had told him many times how they had found him on the side of the road there. She had even pointed out the exact spot where he was lying. Usually, Ezra would stop and stare at the surroundings and ask God to someday show him why he had been left there and why God had allowed the camel driver to find him. He knew this was for a purpose, but he wasn't sure what that purpose was.

His mother and father taught him to trust the True God, and he did. They told him that they had explored all the religions of the world because of their many travels, and it was the God of Israel that proved to them He was the True God. Once they found Him, they had never looked anywhere else for any other god. So, Israel became an even more special place to Ezra.

Because he was so fascinated with Jerusalem, Hebrew was the first language that Ezra learned after his native Babylonian language. His parents were amazed at how easily Ezra learned Hebrew, and afterward, when they encouraged Ezra to learn other languages, it wasn't long before Ezra had learned to speak the languages of almost every place that they traveled with their caravans. He learned Assyrian, Egyptian, Greek, and even some Latin. Everywhere they went, Ezra could interpret for them, and this made Bendar the most sought-after camel driver in all of Babylonia.

Caravans were made up mostly of merchants taking goods for sale to other countries or bringing goods back that they had traded for, which meant three types of camels were needed. One was for the merchants to ride on. Another was for the goods that they carried. The third type of camel needed to be fast and strong because they would be ridden by armed men who guarded the caravans. And because the merchants, guards, and camel drivers all had to be fed, much food and water needed to be packed to eat and drink along the way, requiring even more camels.

Fortunately, they didn't have to carry food or water for the camels, as the camel drivers knew where the oases were. There, they would find all of the water and food that a camel needed for a long journey. Unlike other pack animals, camels can go days and days between when they eat and drink. The men and women along on the trips, on the other hand, had to eat and drink every day.

Usually Ezra's family would provide twenty-four camels for the caravan that they joined. In addition, Bendar, Marca, and Ezra each rode their own special camels, and they had one for their tents and cooking utensils.

Ezra's job was to see to it that each camel was in just the right place. He knew which ones were the strongest, which were the

fastest, which liked to carry people, which did not like carrying people, and where the camels liked to be in the order of the caravan. In short, Ezra was becoming the perfect camel driver's helper.

One day, after a particularly long journey, the family was back in Nippur, resting the camels. As usual, Ezra was tending to the chore of taking care of them.

"Ezra, that camel surely looks ready to me," Marca said. "I know it hasn't been enough time, but her belly is so big she looks like she is giving birth to an elephant rather than a camel."

Ezra smiled to himself. He knew their camels better than anyone. After all, he had been taking care of them for as long as he could remember. He knew each of their names, where they liked to take a snooze, which of the other camels they liked and which they didn't want to be around, and even what each of them liked best to eat. That last piece of knowledge was actually quite a feat, since camels eat almost everything.

In the case of the camel named Bernita, he was pretty sure she was carrying two babies. It was almost unheard of since camels usually only have one calf. He told his mother and father this, but they didn't believe him, since all of the births they had seen over the years had been single calves. But Ezra had been doing the deliveries himself for the past five or six years, and he was pretty sure this one would be different.

Ezra had been watching Bernita carefully for the past few weeks, and his mother was actually right. Bernita was nearing her time. He could tell—not just because of how big she was but because for the past week or so, Bernita had been wandering off into the desert looking for a private place to give birth. Camels don't like to give birth around people, nor even around other camels, so they look for a place where they can be alone for the big event.

"Mother," Ezra said at dinner that night. "I'm sure Bernita has picked out her special place, so if she goes there tonight, I'm going to follow her to be sure she is all right."

"Okay," his mother said. "But you be careful. You know when a camel gives birth the wild dogs can smell it a mile away, and they would like nothing better than to carry off a newborn calf."

"I'll be careful," Ezra said. "And I'll take along my sling and my long knife just in case."

After everyone had finished eating and had retired for the night into the tents, Ezra went out and sat on a big rock where he could look down on all the camels that were gathered around the waterhole in their camp. Ezra's father had chosen this place long ago as their home since it was close to the main road out of Babylon and near an oasis where good, clean water came out of the ground from the faraway mountains. The water nourished the date palms and formed a pool that provided cactus, rushes, and a wide variety of vegetation that gave the camels high-quality nourishment. His father had been a camel driver all his life, so he was an expert in locating just the right place to raise camels.

As for Ezra, he had been around the camels so much that they were almost like family to him. And this particular night, he was going to make sure that he was there for the soon-to-be mother, Bernita, when she might need help and protection.

There was a full moon that night, and the stars were extra bright. The air had a chill to it, so Ezra wrapped his cloak tightly around his shoulders to keep from shivering. Then he lay back against the trunk of a tree to rest—only for a few minutes. Unfortunately, he fell asleep.

All of a sudden, a noise woke him up. With a start, he looked down to where Bernita had been standing. But she was missing. He leaped up as fast as he could and went down the hill on a run. He didn't need to follow Bernita's trail, as he pretty much knew where she was going. After ten minutes of trudging through the scrub oak, the tall reeds beside the pool, and the outcropping of rocks, he came on a short path from the water to an overhang of rock that he knew would provide safety on three sides and shelter from the direct sun in the hot part of the day.

Sure enough, standing there with her head down toward the ground was Bernita. And just at the end of her nose was a small calf that she was licking clean. Right next to that calf was a second calf.

She had, in fact, given birth to twins.

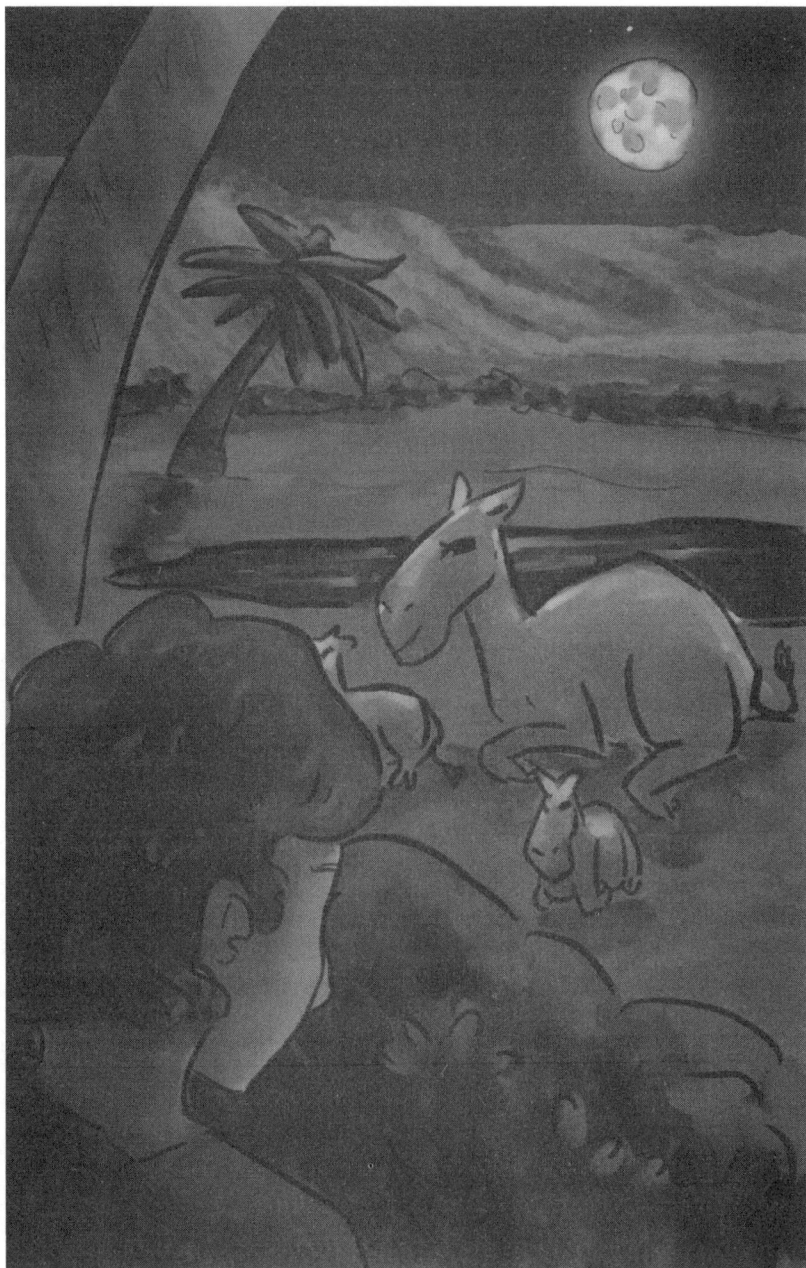

Chapter 3

❊

As Ezra approached the camels, he noticed a couple of things. First, the calves were desperately small. So small that they looked like they might not be able to rise up. And they looked unusually weak. Ezra decided that he would help them stand up so they could be sure to find the way to their mother's milk. Bernita didn't make any protective movements toward Ezra, partly because she was so used to him but also because she could tell he was trying to help.

Ezra reached down for the first calf, putting his hands under the calf's belly to lift it up. At first, the calf didn't know what to do and just let its legs dangle down instead of stiffening its legs to stand up. So every time Ezra lowered the calf to the ground, its legs simply collapsed, and the calf fell down. It took Ezra six or seven times lifting each of the calves before they started supporting themselves and realized they could walk. He was quite relieved that they finally stood on their own because lifting them with only one full arm and his special tool was quite a chore.

The second thing Ezra noticed was that they didn't seem to know where to find their mother, even though she was right next to them. He had to guide each one of them to the place under their mother's belly where they could draw their mother's milk. As he looked more closely at each calf to see if he could tell whether there was anything wrong with them, he saw that they both had one eye closed. He thought that their eyelids must be stuck shut, but when he lifted each offending eyelid, there was no question: both camels were blind in one eye. One was blind in its right eye, and the other was blind in its left eye.

So, when he stepped back to look at what was before him, he saw that Bernita had birthed small, weak, and half-blind twin camels. And he immediately felt a kinship with these new babies. They were disabled just like he was. He proposed right then and there that he would do whatever he could to help these twin camels be all the camel they could be, and he prayed that God would allow this to happen. After he had finished praying, he was sure that God had a special purpose for these twins. And Ezra realized it was up to him to get them ready for whatever that purpose would be.

Over the next year, Ezra spent all his spare time training the twins. One he named Jameen because that means "right" in the Babylonian language, and the calf was blind in his right eye. Ezra named the other, the one who was blind in his left eye, Jassar, which means "left" in the Babylonian language.

To keep them from stumbling off the path or into an obstacle, he taught the camels to always walk side by side with their blind eyes toward each other. In this way, Jameen always walked on the left side and Jassar on the right side.

Bendar was very pleased with the progress that these camels made because for the first time, he could suspend a harness between the two small camels, and they could pull a cart or carry a load together. None of his other camels could do that, as none of his camels were pleased at all to be tied to another camel. Also, the size of the small twins meant that the smaller and more delicate passengers could be more comfortable riding a smaller camel. So many of the women in the caravan were very pleased with the ride.

Many times, Bendar told his son that he appreciated all of Ezra's hard work with the twin camels, as they were almost as good as the big camels. Ezra was quick to disagree with his father. He said that, no, the twins weren't just as good as a large camel—they were better than a large camel. Furthermore, "God has a special plan for these twins, and someday we will all know what it is, and we'll all praise God together because of it," he said.

Most caravans of merchants consisted of one hundred or more camels. This was for protection from bandits who would rob and steal the goods on a caravan if they could. So Bendar, Marca, and Ezra, with their two dozen or so camels, were usually part of a much bigger group as they traveled to so many exotic places. Ezra may have had only one good arm, but he was strong, and he had learned to use his special tool almost as good as a person with two full arms. He was also very good with his sling and his spear when it came to protecting the camels at night from predators.

One day, after arriving home from an especially long and difficult journey, Ezra noticed a commotion at the door of his father's tent. Several men were speaking to Bendar, moving their arms and their hands around excitedly and acting as if there was something very special happening. Clearly, they wanted Bendar to understand whatever it was they were saying. They talked like that for at least an hour before they finally left on the road to Babylon. Ezra wanted to see if his father would come and tell him what the fuss was all about, but Bendar only went back into his tent by himself.

At dinner that night around the fire, Ezra finally asked his father what the three men wanted. But his father would only say that the men had made a request that he wasn't sure his family should be involved in. He told Ezra not to worry about it any further and provided no more details.

Later, Ezra decided he just had to find out what this mysterious request was all about. He knew the men could not have gone all the way back to Babylon that night since they had left the campsite so late. There was an inn not far from the oasis, and Ezra was sure that if he went to the inn, he could find the men and they could tell him what all the excitement was about. So, off he went to the inn.

When he got there, he saw the men sitting around a fire outside the inn, talking to three other men who had not been outside his father's tent that afternoon. Ezra crept up to a rock near the fire where he could hide and listen to what they were saying. They had clearly come outside to talk because they thought no one would be able to hear them. Each group of men was telling the other their story.

And the story that they told was unlike anything Ezra had ever heard.

Chapter 4

O ne man, who seemed to be the leader of their group, started talking.

"I am Muktar Ahmed Zanzzar, of the Royal Priesthood of Nebuchadnezzar, of the Temple of the True God in Babylon. As you know, Nebuchadnezzar was the mighty king of Babylon who built the fabulous Hanging Gardens, who conquered all of the then-known world, whose word was the law, and who seemed invincible. That is until he was brought low by the True God's command, and he was driven out into the fields to live like a common beast. While in this desperate condition, he discovered the One True God and vowed to serve Him and only Him. God restored Nebuchadnezzar to his former glory, and from that day forward until he left the earth, Nebuchadnezzar declared that we should only 'praise the Most High God, the One who lives forever, and whose ways are just.'

"So many years after that, there have been a few in Babylon who continue to follow Nebuchadnezzar's instructions and also follow the One True God. I have been one of those men, as have my friends here who are before you tonight. I give you

Omar Emad Balthazzar." And with that, Ezra saw Zanzzar sit down and Balthazzar stand up in his place and begin talking.

"For many years, our priesthood has studied everything we can about the One True God. Much of what we know has come down from the man who was second in Nebuchadnezzar's kingdom, who was known as Daniel. Daniel interpreted a dream Nebuchadnezzar had that predicted the earthly kingdoms to come, all of which have come true. Babylon fell to the Medes and the Persians. Then came the Greeks who ruled for years and years. And, finally, the Romans came, who rule today. Our priesthood has decided that if Daniel was right about that much of history before it happened, then his last prediction must also come to pass."

"And what is that prediction?" one of the men listening asked.

"Daniel said that God would set up a final kingdom that would never be destroyed and would crush all other kingdoms and last forever."

"That sounds like Rome," one of the other listeners said. "No kingdom is as powerful as Rome."

"But Rome lacks a significant part of the rest of Daniel's prophecy," Balthazzar said. "Rome does not honor the One True God; in fact, Rome has hundreds of gods. And Rome does not give glory to God, the Creator, but only gives glory to itself."

Then Zanzzar stood up again and said, "There is a bigger reason we have asked you to meet us here. We know you are the leaders of our priesthood in the southern regions of Babylon, just as we are the leaders of the northern regions. So we want you to know what we have seen, and we want to know if you have seen it, too, or at least if you agree with us about our response to what we have seen."

"Tell them," Zanzzar said to the third man, who was with him and Balthazzar. The third man stood up and started talking.

"I am Barak Abu Darbarom, the oldest of the priests in our community and the first to have seen the Miracle."

"What do you mean, 'Miracle,' " one of the listeners said.

"Let me explain. I had been led by God to fast and pray for forty days and nights. I didn't know why, but as I obeyed Him, and the days went by, I felt an anticipation that something great was about to happen. On the fortieth night, I knew it was happening, and I wanted my friends here to join me. And, sure enough, while we were kneeling and praying, all the candles in the temple were blown out by a strong wind. Just then, a great light filled the room, and as we huddled in fear, the light flew out of the window and into the night. We were astonished. As one, we ran for the door to see if we could tell where the light had gone.

"When we came out of the east door of the temple, we saw the light in front of us far up in the sky. Then, as if it wanted us to move, it went through the sky to the exact other side of the temple, where it stopped so that it was now due west of where we stood. It stayed there all night. The next day we asked everyone if they had seen the great light, but no one had seen it."

"Every night for the next week, the light appeared, and every day we three came together to study the holy writings of Daniel and of the prophet Isaiah, which have been passed down to us from Daniel's people, the Jews. We studied these to see if we could find the meaning of the great light."

"Had anyone else seen the light?" one of the listeners asked.

"No," Darbarom said. "Only us."

"Did you find out what the light means?" the men asked.

"I can tell you," Zanzzar said. "The Prophet Isaiah said that, 'The people walking in darkness have seen a great light, and on those living in that land of the deep darkness, a great light has dawned.' "

"That's not all," Balthazzar said. "Isaiah also said that, 'Unto us a child is born, and unto us a son is given, and the government will be on his shoulders, and he will be called Mighty God, Everlasting Father, and Prince of Peace.' "

"Don't you see?" he added. "The light we have seen is announcing the coming of the final king that Daniel predicted. The king whose reign will be everlasting and never be destroyed, as Isaiah said. And it can't be Rome. There already have been several Caesars in Rome, and nothing about Rome can be everlasting. Everyone thought the same about Cyrus the Great, and Alexander the Great, and they both are gone, as will Rome be gone one day."

"You better not let the Romans hear you say that," another of the listeners said. "They will throw you in jail."

"What would you have us do?" another listener asked.

"We are going to follow the light to the west, to the land of the Jews, and find this Newborn King. We want to worship him and to bring him gifts. And we would like for you to come with us."

With that, the three listeners said they wanted to talk among themselves before giving their answer. So, they left the fire and huddled near the front wall of the inn. After ten or so minutes, they came back, and one of the three stepped forward to speak.

"I am Cresto, also a member of the Royal Priesthood of Nebuchadnezzar, and speaking for the three of us, I must tell you that none of us has seen the light. We don't doubt that you have seen something that makes you think it is special, but we think if it were a message from the True God, all of us would have seen it. We think you must have been influenced by something in your food or drink. Besides, we have a good relationship with the Roman officials in our area, and we don't want to make them mad by running off to find a new king who is not Roman. So, we are not going with you. We are not going to let anyone see us talking to you. We are leaving now, and if anyone asks us if we have been with you, we are going to deny even having seen you. We think you are on a fool's journey."

And with that, the three of them hurried toward the stable to find their donkeys so they could get away as fast as possible. Darbarom and Balthazzar looked at Zanzzar and said, "What do we do now?"

"It doesn't change a thing," Zanzzar said. "We have been given a great blessing by God, and we can do nothing but follow Him. And that means, we follow the light."

"And how do we start?" Balthazzar said.

"Well, first, we ask the camel driver's helper to come out from behind that rock so we can talk to him," Zanzzar said, without even glancing up at Ezra.

Chapter 5

"How did you know I was hiding here?" Ezra asked, peeking out from behind the rock.

"When we were at your home today, your father pointed you out to us and told us all about how valuable you are as his helper. He also told us how curious a boy you are and how smart you are. Why, he even said you speak most known languages used in the merchants' trade. Is that so?"

"I guess you know that already," Ezra said, "since you are speaking to me in Greek and not the Babylonian language."

"I was just testing you," Zanzzar said.

"And I guess I passed the test," Ezra said. "But how did you know that I was behind the rock?"

"When I was telling the listeners about the light setting in the west, I turned to point that way, and I noticed your coat hanging on the post behind you. It has one long arm and one short arm, so I put two and two together and assumed that someone was behind the rock—someone very curious who was warm

because of the fire and who didn't need his coat until he walked back home in the cool night air. Now, come over here so we can talk to you."

Ezra grabbed his coat and went over to the fire. He was sort of glad they spotted him because he was very interested in hearing more about the great light.

"Did my father say he would take you to Jerusalem?" Ezra asked.

"He hasn't decided yet. He said he wanted to talk to his wife and to you first. There are no other caravans going as far as Jerusalem until spring, so he is afraid of being attacked by bandits if we are so few. What do you think?" Zanzzar asked Ezra.

"It sounds like the most exciting adventure I've ever heard of," he replied.

"What about the danger?" Zanzzar said.

"Well," Ezra said, "if God is telling you to go west and find the Newborn King, don't you think God can protect you from the bandits?"

"You are a wise young man, Ezra. And your father gave you an appropriate name too. Ezra was the prophet who led the Israelites back from Babylon to Jerusalem so many years ago, and now another Ezra will be leading us to Jerusalem," Zanzzar said. "Go back and tell your father that we will return to his house in seven days' time with everything we will need for the trip. If he says he will not lead us, then we will find someone else to receive the blessing of this trip."

With that, Ezra left the fire and hurried home to talk with his mother and father. On the way he thought about all he had been told. And he was convinced that these were the wisest men he had ever met. Surely, he thought, God Himself was the source of that wisdom.

By the time Ezra returned home, his parents were sleeping. So Ezra went to the place where the twins were bedded down for the night, and he piled up some hay so he could be close to them. He always seemed to think best when he was near the twins, and tonight was no different. By morning, he was ready with his arguments to try to convince his father that they should take these Wise Men to Jerusalem.

"Father, I need to talk to you," Ezra said as he came to the table where his mother had set out breakfast.

"Not right now," his father said. "I'm on my way to get some supplies."

"What do you need supplies for?" Ezra asked. "Are we taking a trip this time of year?"

"We certainly are," his father said. "Those three men you saw here yesterday want to go to Jerusalem. Although, I don't see why; there won't be anyone crazy enough to go with us, so we'll be all by ourselves. We will probably be robbed of everything we take, so we won't use the best camels. And, Marca, you are staying here with Ezra so that if anything happens to me, someone will be able to run the camel business. Now, I'll be back in a little while."

Then Bendar rushed off to get supplies while Ezra stood there with his mouth open, not knowing what to say.

"Mother," Ezra said, "I just have to go on this trip."

"Your father doesn't think it is safe," she said.

"But he needs me to take care of the camels and to interpret and to help against any bandits," he said.

"You'll just have to talk to him when he returns," his mother said.

When his father returned, Ezra told him about seeing the men the day before at the inn, and that they were so very wise with all their knowledge of the ancient scriptures. Then he told his father that the Wise Men were coming back in seven days.

"That's good," his father said, since the camels needed their rest from that last trip.

But next Ezra told him that only three men would be coming—not six. His father said that was both good news and bad news. The good news was that they only needed five camels. One for Bendar, one for each of the Wise Men, and the fifth for the supplies. The bad news was that there were fewer of them to fight off any bandits.

Finally, Ezra told his father everything that was said around the campfire about the great light. His father made him repeat the part about the great light twice because he wanted to be sure he heard it correctly. When Ezra again insisted on being allowed to go, rather than simply saying no, his father told him he wanted to think about it for a few days.

During those days, everything proceeded around the camel compound as usual. Ezra gave camels that were hurting some first aid as well as herbs and plants that he knew would help them heal. He trimmed their fur to help keep down the flies and bothersome insects. And he led them to good grazing ground around the clean water. He also repaired the harnesses and the saddles.

Finally, the seventh day arrived, and the Wise Men returned. To prepare for the journey the next day, Bendar told the Wise Men that Ezra wanted to go. Though Bendar was not inclined to let him at first, he had decided he agreed that Ezra should be allowed to come with to Jerusalem.

"What made the decision for you?" Zanzzar asked.

"I prayed for a specific sign," Bendar said. "And God has answered that prayer."

"And what sign was that?" Balthazzar said.

"I asked God to let me see the great light. And right now, I can clearly see it in the west as if it were a great star. But it doesn't rotate like all the other stars; it is fixed, as if to say it is right over the exact place it wants us to be," Bendar said.

"I can see it too," Ezra said, joining the men. And all of them proceeded to praise God and thank Him for this blessing.

The next day, Ezra brought out the camels and they loaded up for their trip. At first, Bendar didn't want Ezra to bring the twins, but Ezra convinced him that he was sure this trip would show them both exactly why it was important for the twins to be along. Ezra didn't know how much this would prove to be true.

The plan Bendar had made for the trip was a simple one. They would avoid towns and villages as much as possible so as to reduce the number of people who were aware of the fact that they were only a small group. Each of the Wise Men and Bendar would have their own camel, and they would carry their own food and water. But the Wise Men wanted to bring the finest robes and headwear and gifts of great value to give to the Newborn King. Bendar had thought they should just bring money and buy what they needed when they arrived in Jerusalem, but the Wise Men insisted that what they were bringing could not be purchased in a marketplace.

So, it was decided that all these special things would be loaded on one of the twins. Bendar thought, in that way, it wouldn't be so obvious that the packages were valuable, for what camel driver in his right mind would put his most valuable goods on such a small and half-blind camel?

Ezra would ride the other twin, as Ezra would have a special job on this trip. One that he was very proud his father trusted him to do.

The small caravan of men on four large camels, small camel loaded with packages wrapped in goat skins, and second small, half-blind camel ridden by a one-armed boy started on the journey that, unknown to them, would be celebrated not only for generations to come, but also in heaven itself.

Chapter 6

{-¦-}

As they went from Nippur around the outskirts of Babylon, Ezra and his camel ran on ahead of the group. He knew the area like the back of his hand, and he, as the scout of the group, was to look for the caves he had used many times on his trips to Babylon for supplies for his family. He went unnoticed through villages and settlements where he was almost a normal sight. No one bothered a lone boy on a small camel.

After a few hours, Ezra found the cave he was looking for partway up a small mountain and hidden from view by a grove of date palm trees. Once he determined that it was empty and the area safe, he went back to find the rest of the group and was able to lead them around the villages right to the safety of the cave.

This method of moving forward in relative safety worked very well for the first two weeks of the trip, but once they were in the Assyrian desert, neither Ezra nor Bendar knew for certain that there were any places of safety where they could hide at night. In addition, there were fewer oases where food for the camels and water for the men were available. So, they were beginning to draw much more attention, and on several days they could see men in the distance watching them as they progressed on their journey.

"Do you think it is safe to have a fire tonight?" Ezra asked after an especially long day of travel.

"We might as well have one," Bendar said. "Those men who have been following us know exactly where we are, anyway, and we need to cook the meat we were able to buy from the last settlement we passed."

"We don't think the men will see us whether we have a fire or not," Zanzzar said.

"Why would you say that?" Ezra asked. "They've seen us all day long, haven't they?"

"Yes," Zanzzar said, "but if they plan to attack us this night, they are in for a big surprise."

"What kind of surprise? And what are you talking about?" Bendar asked.

"We've been reading the ancient Jewish scriptures each morning and each evening," Darbarom said. "And with each danger that seems to come our way, God has given us a scripture that shows us there is a way out for our situation."

"What way out?" Ezra asked.

"In the ancient scriptures, God sent men into a city that He intended to destroy. They were confronted by evil men who intended to do them harm. So, you know what God did?"

"What?" Ezra asked.

"He blinded the evil men so they could not see God's messengers. And we are confident that God will blind these men out in the desert, if necessary, to keep them from harming us," Balthazzar said. And that is exactly what God did. The men never seemed to know exactly where the group was, and they always seemed to be wandering in confusion.

After many days of travel, when they were able to leave the men of Assyria behind, the great light that had been leading them west all of a sudden turned south toward Jerusalem.

"We are entering a very bad area," Bendar said. "From the edge of Assyria to the Sea of Galilee, there are bandits that threaten all caravans. Sometimes they attack and steal everything, including the camels, and just leave all the survivors to walk out of the desert on their own. Most never make it.

"Other times they stop the caravan and demand a ransom to allow the caravan to go through. They are smart enough to know that they gain more by not taking everything because then that caravan will have to come through on its way back, and they can demand a ransom again to allow it to pass."

"What will they do to us, since we are so small?" Ezra asked.

"I don't know," Bendar said. "But we are about to find out, as I see two of the leaders of the bandits coming toward us right now."

"Let me do the talking," Zanzzar said. "God has already answered our prayers for safety, and we need not fear."

Bendar had no idea what Zanzzar was talking about, but he didn't argue. He just stayed with their small group while Zanzzar went out to meet the bandit leaders. From a distance, Ezra could see them talking. He could tell the two bandits were yelling at Zanzzar, who was just sitting on his camel as calm as could be, as if he didn't have a care in the world. Finally, the bandits started riding in circles around Zanzzar several times, swinging their curved blades in the air. Then they went galloping off. Zanzzar returned to the group.

"What did they say?" Bendar asked.

"They said that unless we gave them everything we had, including our camels, they were going to attack and kill us all."

"What did you say?" Ezra asked.

"I told them that they had no power over the messengers of God, and they would be wise to ride away while they still could before the judgement of God came upon them with fire and brimstone."

"Wow," Ezra said. "I wish I could have seen their faces when they heard that."

"Aren't you afraid, Ezra?" Bendar asked.

"No, Father," Ezra said. "I'm not afraid. I'm only anxious to see how God will protect us. I am certain that what God has prepared me to do is yet to come, so I know He will not let any harm come to me until that is accomplished."

That night, and every night and day thereafter, until the small group reached the Sea of Galilee, they could see the whole army of bandits that must have consisted of one hundred men on camels gather in the distance. The men would yell and scream and beat their swords against their shields and charge toward the small group. But they always stopped short and never got closer than a stone's throw away from the group.

"Why do they stop?" Ezra asked.

"It's because we outnumber them and are obviously more powerful," Darbarom said.

"I don't understand," Ezra said. "We are only a few, and we have no weapons to defend ourselves."

"In the ancient scriptures, the prophet Elishia had someone ask him the same question," Zanzzar said. "So, God let him see what his enemies could see. I pray that God would give you the same blessing," he told Ezra.

And just as the Wise Men were moving away, Ezra's eyes were opened, and he saw for the first time hundreds of men in white robes with flaming swords surrounding the Wise Men and the small group. Then he remembered what Zanzzar had read at the campfire weeks ago. "And the angels of the Lord will surround those who love Him and will protect them from harm."

Ezra knew for sure then that they would accomplish what God had planned and no evil would stop them.

Later, after circling the Sea of Galilee, they finally came to Jerusalem.

"We have arrived in the center of the Jewish world, but I don't understand why there isn't a celebration going on for the Newborn King," Darbarom said.

"Surely, everyone knows of his arrival" Balthazzar added. "It is a great event."

"Apparently not," Zanzzar said. "We have asked everyone where he is so we can worship him, and people just look at us like we are crazy."

"Well, the current king seems to know something," Balthazzar said, "as he has sent his soldiers to collect us. From what the soldiers say, King Herod doesn't know what to think about us. So, let's talk to him. Surely, he can tell us where the Newborn King can be found."

"Are you going to wear your finery and show him your gifts?" Ezra asked. "After all, he is still a king in this country."

"No," Zanzzar said. "We all three have been made aware by the Spirit of God that this is not a worthy king, and he is not one to be trusted. We are only going to see what he might know about the Newborn King."

When the Wise Men came back from their visit to King Herod, Bendar and Ezra were full of questions, and the Wise Men were full of answers.

"He doesn't know about the Newborn King. His advisors say that seven hundred years ago, a prophet said that the king described by Daniel and Isaiah would be born in Bethlehem. And King Herod said that if we go there, we might find him. If we do, he wants us to come back and tell him where the Newborn King is living so that he, King Herod, can go out and worship the Jewish King as well. But we don't trust King Herod, and an angel appeared to us in a dream last night who told us that after we find the Newborn King and have given him our gifts, we are to return to Babylon by a different route than the way we came into Jerusalem. In that way, we can avoid King Herod and his men."

As the night grew darker, the great light again appeared, and the Wise Men knew the time had come. They went into their tent, and Ezra could hear them praying out loud and singing hymns and praising God. Then it got quiet in the tent, and Ezra wondered if maybe they had fallen asleep. But after a short time the Wise Men came out of the tent and Ezra and Bendar were speechless. Instead of being dressed in their travel clothes, the Wise Men were dressed in finery that was fit for kings, and Ezra and Bendar knew then that this was to be a special night like no other they had ever experienced.

Chapter 7

Ezra had never seen such splendor. Darbarom had a coat of the finest lambswool dyed a bright green and lined with white fur. It was covered with gold stars and had a red collar of the finest fox fur. Darbarom's head was wrapped with a turban as black as a raven and adorned in the front by a large, red stone that almost glowed as it reflected the great light.

Balthazzar's coat was midnight blue with a yellow collar and cuffs, and it had silver latches across the front to hold it closed. His head was covered with what looked like a round box with a flat top, which was covered in sparkled sequins that reflected the light like hundreds of small stars.

But Zanzzar was the most magnificent of all. He had trousers that were tied at the ankles but were puffed out all the way up to his waist where they were held up by a gold sash tied on the side. His shirtsleeves were also puffed out, from his wrists to his shoulders. Both the trousers and his shirt were red velvet, and around his neck was a sash made from a material Ezra had seen only one time before on a trip to the Far East.

The material was called silk, and it was spun by caterpillars that only lived in one part of the world. Over his shoulders, Zanzzar had a cape that came all the way to his feet in the back. It was a beautiful jet-black color, as was the crown on his head, except that the crown was covered in pearls.

Bendar and Ezra could only stare. The three Wise Men did not speak at all. They retrieved their gifts from the packages on the back of the twin camel, mounted their own camels, and started out following the great light. The golden beam was shining immediately in front of their camels. Bendar and Ezra followed behind at some distance from the Wise Men, but not so far as to lose sight of them. They both knew that this was a night for the Wise Men alone and that they didn't belong alongside of them.

After an hour or so of traveling through the streets of Bethlehem, the great light stopped over the roof of a house at the end of a fairly deserted road. No one seemed to notice either the great light or the Wise Men as they made their way down street after street until they came to the house. It seemed as if God were protecting the Wise Men from any distractions as they made their way to the Newborn King.

The great light lit up the house, the trees around the house, and the whole surrounding area as bright as the sun. The stable beside the house and the path up to it had such a glow that it looked almost brighter than day.

The three Wise Men dismounted their camels and walked up the path with their gifts in their hands. They were greeted at the top of the path by a man, a woman, and a small boy, all of whom sat on the flat rock before the front door of the house. The boy was in the lap of his mother. The three Wise Men kneeled before the boy and uncovered their gifts—gold, frankincense, and myrrh. They were the finest that Bendar and Ezra had ever seen in all their travels.

They stayed with the couple and the boy for more than an hour. Then they rose up, and, while still bowing, they backed down the path to where Bendar and Ezra were holding the camels. "We can now go back to Babylon, praising God and rejoicing for the great gift God has given to us and to all mankind. And we will tell our followers we've seen the Newborn King prophesied by Daniel and Isaiah, and that Immanuel has said that God is now among us."

"We can leave first thing in the morning," Bendar said.

"No," Zanzzar said. "We need to leave now. As we said, we have been warned in a dream to get away from King Herod as soon as we can without any delay."

Just then Ezra said to his father, "I can't go. I need to stay here."

"That's foolish," Bendar said. "Why would you do that?"

"Father," he said, "I can feel it in my bones that God is not finished with me yet on this trip."

"Well, He can finish with you in Babylon," Bendar said.

"No," Balthazzar said. "I think Ezra is right. I think God has something for him to do."

"I can't imagine what that could be," Bendar said. "I can't just leave you here alone. Your mother would never forgive me."

"I will be all right," Ezra said. "Didn't you see how God blinded the bandits and protected us with the men with flaming swords? And didn't God lead us here with the great light?"

"Of course," Bendar said.

"Well, He won't stop taking care of me now, as long as I'm doing His will. And I'm sure my staying here is in His will."

After more discussion, and after Bendar shed tears, he held his son and said, "God go with you, my son. And I am leaving the twins with you. I'm sure they won't mind me, anyway, and perhaps they will keep you company until we meet again."

"We will meet again, Father," Ezra said. "I'm sure of it."

As the Wise Men and Bendar rode off into the night and Ezra watched, he felt a tap on his shoulder. It was the man from the house.

"Hello," he said. "I'm Joseph, and this is my wife, Mary, and we saw that you and your twin camels have stayed behind. Instead of standing here in the cold, why don't you come on up and spend the night in the stable?"

"I would appreciate that very much," Ezra said.

And after caring for the twins, Ezra lay down on a pile of straw and was soon fast asleep.

It seemed like no time at all when he awoke to a bright sunrise. As he rose to check on the twins, he heard a commotion coming from the front porch of the house. Approaching, he heard an old woman crying and talking. "You need to go," she said. "You need to hide. The soldiers are coming, and King Herod has ordered that all boys under two years of age must be put to death. You need to take your child and run."

With that, she turned and ran down the path, crying, "I need to warn the others. I need to warn the others."

"What will we do?" Mary asked Joseph.

"We will go to Egypt," Joseph said. "An angel appeared to me to warn me of this tragedy and said that we must stay in Egypt until the danger passes over."

"But how will we get there?" Mary asked.

"I know how you will get there," Ezra blurted out. "I'll take you there. I just knew God had a plan for me and for my twin camels. And now I see clearly what that plan is. I have been to Egypt many times. I speak the language. My twin camels are strong and can easily carry the two of you, and I can walk miles every day. I've been doing it all my life."

Then he looked down at the ground and added softly, "The only thing you might think are problems are that I only have one good arm, and the twin camels are both blind in one eye."

Mary and Joseph just smiled at each other, and then they smiled at Ezra.

"Don't worry, Ezra, we would be honored for you to take us to Egypt," Joseph said.

"And it is exciting for us, Ezra," Mary said, also calling him by his name, "because then God will be using the weak and disabled of

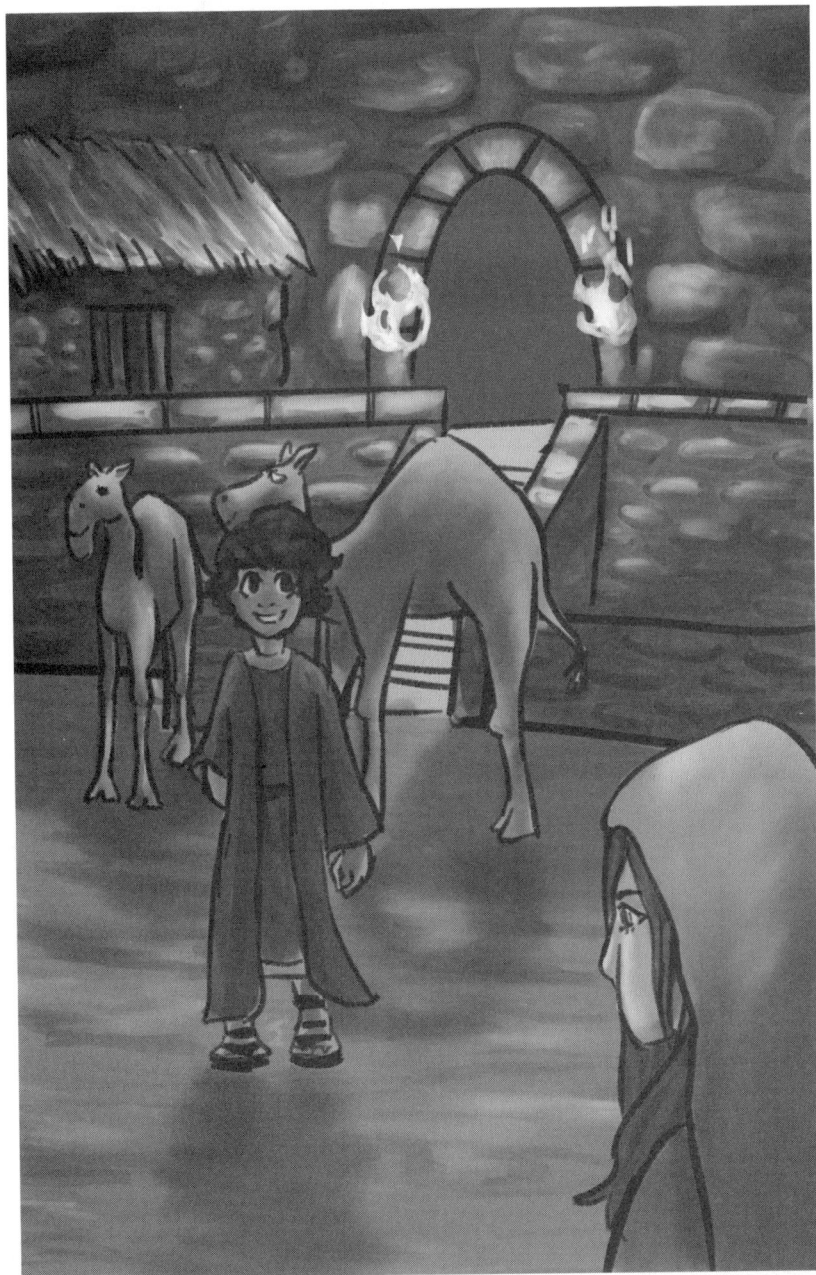

this world to help our baby, Jesus. This will confound those who think they are smart and strong but who are really the ones who are weak, blind, and deaf."

"You can always be sure, Ezra," she added, "if God calls you to do it, He will bring you through it. And it is clear God has prepared you and your twin camels for a time such as this."

"Let us get our things, and we will join you, our new friend, on this amazing journey," Joseph said.

And what an amazing journey it was for Joseph, the carpenter; Mary, the mother of Jesus; Jesus, the Son of God; Ezra, the one-armed camel driver's helper; and two half-blind camels.

About the Author

Terry Parker was a longtime friend of Larry Burkett, who was heard on over a thousand radio stations with his program *Christian Financial Concepts*. After Larry's death, Terry formed the Larry Burkett Cancer Research Foundation and has written under the pen name GrandDad three other books in a series he calls the Robert P. Rabbit books. These books are primarily given away as an encouragement to children with cancer and other disabilities. Any income from the sale of this book will be used to pay for additional books to be given to cancer camps, children's hospitals, Ronald McDonald Houses, and other places where children with illnesses are ministered to.

Terry is an attorney who retired as a senior partner of a five-hundred-member law firm he was with for twenty-eight years. He is a cofounder of the National Christian Foundation with Larry Burkett and Ron Blue.